A Note to Parents and Caregivers:

Read-it! Readers are for children who are just starting on the amazing road to reading. These beautiful books support both the acquisition of reading skills and the love of books.

 The PURPLE LEVEL presents basic topics and objects using high frequency words and simple language patterns.

 The RED LEVEL presents familiar topics using common words and repeating sentence patterns.

 The BLUE LEVEL presents new ideas using a larger vocabulary and varied sentence structure.

 The YELLOW LEVEL presents more challenging ideas, a broad vocabulary, and wide variety in sentence structure.

 The GREEN LEVEL presents more complex ideas, an extended vocabulary range, and expanded language structures.

 The ORANGE LEVEL presents a wide range of ideas and concepts using challenging vocabulary and complex language structures.

When sharing a book with your child, read in short stretches, pausing often to talk about the pictures. Have your child turn the pages and point to the pictures and familiar words. And be sure to reread favorite stories or parts of stories.

There is no right or wrong way to share books with children. Find time to read with your child, and pass on the legacy of literacy.

Adria F. Klein, Ph.D.
Professor Emeritus
California State University
San Bernardino, California

To my children, Ryan and Katy, a source of delight in my life—Jennifer Guess McKerley

Editor: Shelly Lyons
Designer: Hilary Wacholz
Page Production: Ashlee Schultz
Art Director: Nathan Gassman
Associate Managing Editor: Christianne Jones
The illustrations in this book were created with watercolor,
colored pencil, and digital mediums.

Picture Window Books
5115 Excelsior Boulevard
Suite 232
Minneapolis, MN 55416
877-845-8392
www.picturewindowbooks.com

Printed in the United States of America.

All books published by Picture Window Books
are manufactured with paper containing at least
10 percent post-consumer waste.

Library of Congress Cataloging-in-Publication Data
McKerley, Jennifer Guess.
There goes Turtle's hat / by Jennifer Guess McKerley ; illustrated by
Andi Carter.
  p. cm. — (Read-it! readers)
  ISBN 978-1-4048-4327-1 (library binding)
  [1. Turtles—Fiction. 2. Hats—Fiction. 3. Zoo animals—Fiction.
4. Stories in rhyme.] I. Carter, Andi, 1976- ill. II. Title.
PZ8.3.M4597Th 2008
[E]—dc22   2007032900

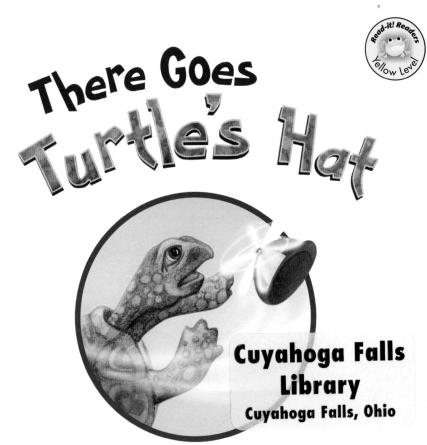

There Goes Turtle's Hat

Read-it! Readers
Yellow Level

Cuyahoga Falls
Library
Cuyahoga Falls, Ohio

by Jennifer Guess McKerley
illustrated by Andi Carter

Special thanks to our reading adviser:

Adria F. Klein, Ph.D.
Professor Emeritus, California State University
San Bernardino, California

PICTURE WINDOW BOOKS
Minneapolis, Minnesota

One day, the wind blew Turtle's hat. The hat sailed away, just like that.

It floated over to the zoo and stopped atop
a kangaroo.

7

The kangaroo sneezed, and off it flew, out of the pen and around the zoo.

9

It landed in the lion's den. A lion's tail swished and made it spin!

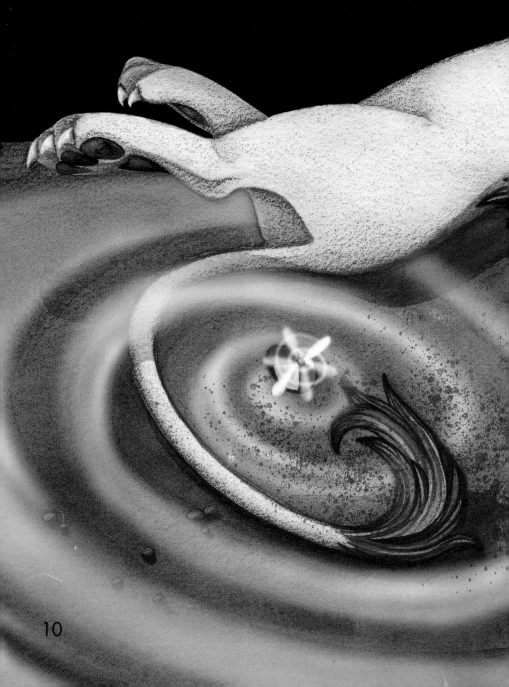

11

Turtle looked high.

Turtle looked low. He asked, "My favorite hat, where did it go?"

The hat blew here.

14

The hat blew there, over the seal and around the bear.

The ape tried to grab it. The rhino tried to jab it.

The moose tried to stomp it. The giraffe tried to chomp it.

It zigged. It zagged. It zipped.
It dipped.

Turtle's hat had quite a trip!

It landed beside a big old gnu. She told Turtle,
"You must use glue!"

Now when the wind blows Turtle's hat, off he sails, just like that.

23

More *Read-it!* Readers

Bright pictures and fun stories help you practice your reading skills.
Look for more books at your level.

Benny and the Birthday Gift
The Best Lunch
The Boy Who Loved Trains
Car Shopping
Clinks the Robot
Firefly Summer
The Flying Fish
Gabe's Grocery List
Loop, Swoop, and Pull!
Patrick's Super Socks
Paulette's Friend

Pony Party
Princess Bella's Birthday Cake
The Princesses' Lucky Day
Rudy Helps Out
The Sand Witch
Say "Cheese"!
The Snow Dance
The Ticket
Tuckerbean at Waggle World
Tuckerbean in the Kitchen

On the Web

FactHound offers a safe, fun way to find Web sites related to topics
in this book. All of the sites on FactHound have been researched
by our staff.

1. Visit *www.facthound.com*

2. Type in this special code:
   1404843272

3. Click on the FETCH IT button.

Your trusty FactHound will fetch the best sites for you!
A complete list of *Read-it!* Readers is available on our Web site:
www.picturewindowbooks.com